# Old Ruff and Life on the Farm

*Vesta Seek*
*Illustrated by*
*Nancy Munger*

Chariot Books™ is an imprint of David C. Cook Publishing Co.
David C. Cook Publishing Co., Elgin, Illinois 60120
David C. Cook Publishing Co., Weston, Ontario
Nova Distribution Ltd., Newton Abbot, England



Art Direction by Dawn Lauck
First Printing, 1993
Printed in Singapore
97 96 95 94 93 5 4 3 2 1

**Library of Congress Cataloging-in-Publication Data**
Seek, Vesta
Old Ruff and life on the farm/by Vesta Seek
p. cm. —(An on my own book)
Summary: With God's help, Janie trains Ruff to be a good dog and refrain from chasing the cows on her farm.
ISBN 0-7814-0966-7
[1. Dogs—Fiction. 2. Farm life—Fiction. 3. Christian life—Fiction.] I. Title. II. Series
PZ7.S45160k 1993
[E]—dc20 92-12956
CIP
AC

Ruff was a very little dog
when he first came to the farm.
"Oh, Pa," said Janie
to her father.
"What a dear little dog.
What is his name?"
"I don't know," laughed Pa.
"I guess he has no name."

Just then, Ma, Janie's mother,

came out of the house.

When she saw the little dog,

she said, "Well, well.

Who is this?"

The little dog looked at Ma.

"Ruff, ruff," he barked.

"Funny little dog," said Janie.

"Is your name Ruff, ruff?"

The little dog jumped at something

in the grass.

"Ruff, ruff," he barked again.

They all laughed.

"Let's call him 'Ruff,' " said Janie.

"Yes," said Pa and Ma.

"That is a very good name

for a very good little dog."

“Now we must work with Ruff,”

said Pa.

“We want him to come when we call,

and he must not

make the cows run.”

"I have so much farm work to do,"

said Pa.

"Janie, do you think you can

work with Ruff?"

"I will try," said Janie.

"And I will ask God to help me.

I think it will be fun!"

Ma and Janie talked to God.

"Dear God, please help me work with Ruff so he can be a good farm dog," prayed Janie.

"Amen," they said.

They put a rope on the little dog.

When he went out in the grass, Janie said, "Come," and she pulled on the rope.

She pulled the little dog

up to her.

“Ruff, ruff,” he barked.

Then Janie gave him

a little cookie.

“Good dog,” she said.

She did this over and over,

day after day.

One day, Janie and the little dog
walked out in the big field.
“I think you want to go
for a long run,” said Janie.
So she took off the rope
and let him go.

But there was something

Janie did not see.

Cows were sleeping

way down by the fence.

Pa had just put up that fence.

He was happy with his new fence.

All at once, Ruff saw the cows!

*What is this?* he thought.

*Here is something big*

*for me to play with!*

He ran right up to the cows.

"Ruff, ruff!" he barked.

"Bow-wow-wow!"

"Oh! NO! NO!" cried Janie.

"COME! COME!

COME, Ruff!

Come away from

the cows.

Come! Please come!"

But it was too late!

When the cows saw the dog,

they jumped up.

They wanted to run away,

But where could they go?

All the cows ran

right into the fence,

and down it came!

“Oh, my!” cried Janie.

“Now what can I do?”

Janie ran and got Ruff.

Then she ran to the house

as fast as she could.

“Pa! Oh, Pa!” she cried.

But Pa was not there.

Ma and Janie's brothers

came running.

"What is it?" they asked.

"What is it?"

"Oh, please help me!" cried Janie.

"The fence is down

and the cows are out!"

Janie put little Ruff

in the barn.

Ma and the brothers went

and got the cows.

Then they worked to get

the fence back up.

“Maybe we will not tell Pa

about this,” they said.

“He liked his new fence so much.

It looks pretty good now.

Maybe he will never know it was down.”

But Pa saw it the very next day.

“Oh! Oh!” he said.

“Something is not right here!

My fence was not like this!”

So Janie had to tell Pa

all about it. . . .

"Well, well," said Pa.

"That's too bad.

But we cannot have a dog

that makes the cows run.

It is not good for them.

I guess we cannot keep

that little dog."

“Oh dear,” said Janie.

“Why did the cows run like that?

This dog is so little.

He cannot hurt the cows.

Why did they run, Pa?”

"I don't know, Janie," answered Pa.

"But cows are like that.

When the little dog said, 'Ruff! Ruff!'

and ran at them,

they wanted to get away fast.

Cows are like that!"

"Oh, Pa," said Janie,

"little Ruff likes it here.

I think he can learn.

Please, Pa, let me try

to help him."

Pa looked at Janie.

She looked so sad.

“Well, all right,” said Pa.

“I will let you try again.

But if Ruff runs the cows

one more time,

then he must go.”

“Oh, thank you, Pa,” said Janie.

“I will work with him every day.

I will ask God to help me.”

Janie put the rope on Ruff

and went near the cows.

"Ruff! Ruff!" said the dog.

But Janie said, "No! No!"

and pulled him away.

Every day for days and days

she did this.

When Ruff saw cows, all he thought was,

*No! No! No!*

One night in bed,

Janie was thinking

about her little dog.

“I don’t like to say no to him,

but I love him.

I want to help him.

That is why I say no so much.”

Janie thought about Ma and Pa.

"Sometimes they say no to me.

Now I see why they do it.

They love me.

They want to help me."

Janie lay very still.

Then softly she said,

"Dear God, You are like that.

You love me. You want to help me.

Sometimes You say no.

But You always know

what's best for me.

Thank You, God. I love You so much."

The next morning, Pa took Ruff

out in the big field

with no rope on him.

*Oh, dear,* thought Janie.

*What will Ruff do?*

*I will not be there*

*to say no to him!*

Pa and Ruff were away

for a long time!

But when they came back,

Pa had a happy face.

Janie ran to him.

"This dog is okay," said Pa.

"He will stay here and be

our good farm dog!"

What a happy day for Janie!

Ruff was happy too.

He lived at the farm

for a long, long time.

The family all loved him.

They called him

*Good Old Ruff.*

And he never, ever

made the cows run again.